THE STAR BEYOND THE RUINS

AMIT SONAR

Contents

Foreword

We all build walls. Sometimes it's to protect ourselves. Sometimes it's just to survive. I didn't start writing this book because I had some big, romantic idea to share. Honestly, it was the opposite. I wrote it because I had spent a long time feeling... numb. Detached. Like I was just going through the motions, trying not to feel too much, because feeling had hurt me before.

This isn't just a story about love it's about what happens when you spend so long shutting out the world, only to have someone walk in and gently, quietly, remind you what it means to feel again.

It's about a guy who believed that the safest way to live was to stay guarded. Someone who thought that if he could just control everything, his thoughts, his emotions, his heart. He wouldn't have to hurt again. But then someone showed up who didn't try to fix him. She didn't force her way in. She just stayed. And in the stillness between them, something began to change.

If you've ever buried your feelings because you thought they were too heavy to carry...

If you've ever looked calm on the outside but felt like you were falling apart inside...

If you've ever been scared to open up, to trust, to love again...

Then maybe this story is for you.

Writing this helped me understand that healing doesn't always come in big, dramatic moments. Sometimes it shows up in a shared silence, a small smile, a simple presence that makes the air feel lighter. And sometimes, just sometimes, the scariest thing feeling again is exactly what we need the most.

I hope, as you read this, you find a little bit of yourself in these pages. And I hope it reminds you, gently, that it's okay to feel again. Even if it hurts. Especially if it hurts.

Preface

This book began as a way to process emotions I didn't know how to express out loud. It started with scattered thoughts, pieces of memory, and questions I had no answers to. Over time, those fragments shaped themselves into a story, a story that, while fictional, carries truth in every line.

At its core, this is a journey of a man learning how to feel again. He isn't a hero. He isn't trying to save the world. He's just someone who, like many of us, got hurt deeply and decided that feeling nothing was safer than feeling everything. This is about what happens when that belief is challenged slowly, unexpectedly, and profoundly by someone who sees him, really sees him, even when he can't see himself clearly.

I didn't write this for happy endings. I wrote it to honor the moments in between the quiet, complicated ones where growth happens, often without us realizing it. Where we discover that vulnerability isn't weakness, and that love, in its purest form, doesn't try to fix you; it simply stands beside you, offering warmth in a world that sometimes feels cold.

This isn't a guidebook or a fairy tale. It's just a story, honest, raw, and, I hope, relatable.

If you've ever carried invisible scars, stayed silent when you wanted to scream, or shut the door on your own heart just to survive, this book is for you.

It's not about how we fall, it's about what we choose to do after we hit the ground.

Acknowledgements

This book was born from real moments, quiet reflections, and the kind of growth that only life can teach. It wasn't easy to revisit the memories that shaped these pages, but doing so helped me understand more about myself and the quiet shifts that make us who we are.

To my family, thank you for your constant love and patience, even when I couldn't always express what I was carrying. Your support was the quiet strength behind every word.

To my friends, the ones who stood by me, reminded me to breathe, and never made me feel alone, thank you for simply being there. Your presence meant more than you'll ever know.

This book is also for anyone who's struggled to find peace within themselves. Writing this helped me better understand how self-growth changes us—not just how we think, but how we feel, how we connect, and how we learn to open up again.

Thank you to those who unknowingly became a part of this journey, whose moments, words, and silences left echoes in these pages.

With a humble heart,
-Amit Sonar

Prologue

Life does not warn you how it will change you. Sometimes it feels like it is gently shaping you, like a stone smoothed by water, and sometimes it hits you so hard you do not even know where the cracks started. I did not know what would break inside me until it happened. This story is about a man who had learned to navigate life with a sharp sense of practicality. To him, emotions were variables best kept in check, controlled and measured, because they had once brought him to his knees. His heart had been battered and bruised by a past that taught him one cruel truth: hope could betray you, love could abandon you, and trust could be the sharpest knife of all.

For years, he lived under the illusion that detachment was survival. His world was small, meticulously arranged. Every piece had its place, and his heart, wounded but still beating, was carefully locked away. He had no room for unnecessary risks, no space for unpredictable joys or heartaches. In his mind, life was about staying afloat, keeping to safe waters, and avoiding the tempest that love could bring.

Then, unexpectedly, he met her.

It was not one of those sweeping, cinematic encounters where two souls collide in a moment of destiny. It was something quieter, yet far too powerful. She entered his life like a melody that sneaks into your mind and lingers there, familiar and beautiful. There was nothing extraordinary about the way they met, just a simple crossing of paths, an unremarkable introduction. But something stirred within him, a flicker of recognition in a part of himself he thought had long since gone dark.

She was different from anyone he had known. Her laugh was not loud or dramatic, but it had a way of making the quiet feel less cold. When she was around, it was like the air got a little easier to breathe. She did not make things better, but in some small way, she made me feel less alone. She was warmth in a world he had grown used to seeing in shades of gray. She was not afraid to speak her mind or to sit in the quiet moments without filling the space with words. Her honesty cut through his cynicism, her openness challenged his need for control. And with her, he found himself questioning everything he thought he knew about love, vulnerability, and happiness.

She did not try to fix him. She did not ask him to change. Instead, she simply existed, steadfast and certain in her own imperfect way. Her stories, filled with humor and heartbreak, made him realize how much he had been missing by shutting the world out. She had her own scars, her own burdens, but she carried them with grace and an unspoken resilience that both inspired and terrified him.

In her, he saw a reflection of his own struggles. But where he had chosen to build walls, she had chosen to grow gardens. She had faced darkness too, but instead of retreating, she planted seeds of hope. It was not that she was unafraid of being hurt, she simply refused to let fear dictate her life. It was this quiet defiance, this refusal to grow bitter, that captivated him completely.

For the first time in what felt like forever, he allowed himself to feel. It started with small cracks in his armor, an irresistible smile at her jokes, a late-night conversation that stretched into dawn, a glance held a second too long. It happened slowly, so gradually that he did not even notice until one day he realized he was not holding himself back as much. And that scared him. He had spent years building walls, making sure nothing could get too close. But then it started to feel okay, and that was even scarier. Because feeling something, really feeling it, meant he might lose it again.

Yet love, like a gentle breeze, can make you shiver to the core. He wrestled with the demons of his past, the memories of betrayal and loss that whispered caution into his ear. Every time he felt himself leaning closer, he heard the voice of his younger self warning him, Remember what happened before. Remember how it felt when everything fell apart.

She was not perfect. None of us are. But she was patient, in a way that made him wonder how she could stay so calm when he was falling apart inside. She did not rush him, did not make him feel like he had to be someone he was not. It was not about fixing him, it was about letting him figure it out in his own time. Somehow, that made it easier for him to let the walls down.

This is a story of transformation, of a man who believed that safety lay in solitude, only to discover that true strength comes from connection. It is about the journey from self-imposed isolation to the openness of love, a love that does not seek to complete, but to complement, to stand side by side rather than fill empty spaces.

It is about those unexpected moments that force us to confront our deepest fears and greatest desires. The way one person can walk into our lives and change everything, not by offering answers, but by reminding us of the questions worth asking. It is about learning that vulnerability is not weakness, but courage in its purest form.

This is for anyone who has ever built walls to protect themselves, for those who have locked their hearts away in fear of the pain that love can bring. This story is a reminder that beyond those walls lies a world full of possibility. Yes, there is risk. Yes, there may be pain. But there is also beauty, connection, and a kind of joy that cannot be measured or controlled.

Because sometimes the things that really matter, the things that break us and remake us, are the things we are afraid to even look at. The walls we build to keep us safe can trap us. And the only way out is to let go, to trust that maybe, just maybe, there is something worth risking for.

CHAPTER ONE

WHISPERS OF THE WATERFALL

The rain had been falling gently all morning, casting a silver sheen over the world as Zane and his friends made their way to the famous waterfall just outside the city. The air filled with the thick scent of wet earth and blooming flowers, a fragrant reminder that summer had arrived in full force. They were four friends on a holiday outing, ready to shake off the weight of exams and deadlines in the cool embrace of nature's beauty. The hike up to the waterfall had been full of teasing, lighthearted jabs at each other's exhaustion, and the familiar rhythm of laughter that only the best of friends can create. Zane was grateful for this, the time to clear his mind after weeks of stress.

The waterfall was alive with energy. A curtain of water cascaded from jagged cliffs, crashing into the pool below with a roar that vibrated in Zane's chest and the surrounding area. Around them, clusters of tourists and locals filled the area, their laughter and chatter blending with the relentless rush of the falls. Bright umbrellas dotted the shore like flowers in a garden, and children squealed as they splashed in the shallows. The holiday spirit was infectious, a perfect mix of joy and chaos.

The four friends waded into the water, the chill biting at their skin but refreshing after the hike. Zane let the force of the current push against him as he leaned back, staring up at the sky where clouds hung heavy with rain. His friends were already splashing around, but Zane felt a strange peace in the sound of the waterfall, the world blurring around him as he lost himself in the moment. It was then that he noticed her.

She stood on the edge of the water, her eyes scanning the pool with an inquisitive gleam. Raindrops clung to her dark hair, and her face, open and expressive, carried a kind of unguarded wonder that struck him. She wasn't alone; she had come with a group of family friends, but there was something about her that seemed untethered, as if she belonged more to the world around her than to the people she was with. She stood out from the crowd, her energy different from the rest. Something about her drew his attention in a way that nothing else had.

A moment later, she was in the water, making her way toward them with easy confidence. Her steps sent ripples dancing across the surface as she closed the distance. Zane watched as her smile grew wider, her eyes sparkling with a mix of mischief and warmth. It felt like time slowed down for a moment.

"Hey!" Her voice was bright, cutting through the din of the falls. "You guys having fun?"

They turned as one, surprised but intrigued. Zane couldn't help but feel a small flutter in his chest as their gazes met. She was younger than he, but there was something about her presence that felt familiar, as if they had known each other for far longer than just a few seconds.

"Yeah," Zane said, a grin tugging at his lips. "It's a good day for it."

"I think so too," she replied, her gaze settling on him. "The water's freezing, though!"

"Cold wakes you up," one of his friends chimed in, splashing water playfully toward her.

She laughed, stepping back just in time to avoid the spray. "Oh, I'll remember that next time I need a wake-up call." Her tone was teasing, and her smile was easy. Zane found himself smiling in return, appreciating how naturally she fit into the carefree atmosphere of the moment.

"Where are you from?" another friend asked.

She brushed a strand of wet hair behind her ear. "Not too far. My parents wanted to drag me out of the house today, so here I am." She gestured toward a group on the shore. "Family friends."

"Well, you picked a good spot," Zane said. "This place is kind of magical in the rain."

Her eyes lifted toward the waterfall, her expression softening as she took in the scene. "Yeah. It's beautiful. Like something out of a storybook."

"First time here?" Zane asked, his curiosity piqued.

She nodded, her eyes never leaving the rushing water. "First time, but definitely not the last. I love places like this. It feels alive." She turned to him with a grin. "Do you come here often, or is this a special adventure?"

"A bit of both," Zane said. "We needed a break, and this spot never disappoints."

"It doesn't," she agreed. "Even with all the people, it still feels like you can get lost in it." She tilted her head, studying him. "What do you usually do when you're not here getting?"

"Mostly trying not to drown in textbooks," Zane replied, laughing. "Finals were brutal."

"Oh, I know that feeling." She laughed, a sound that seemed to brighten the overcast day. "I just finished my exams too. The relief is real."

As they continued talking, the sound of the waterfall filling the air around them, Zane casually mentioned his college in a conversation about exams.

"So, you're in school? Where?" Zane asked, intrigued by the ease with which she fit into their conversation.

She raised an eyebrow, clearly curious. "High school," she admitted with a sheepish smile. "For now, anyway. But not for much longer."

Zane's interest piqued. "Moving on to bigger things?" he teased.

She nodded, her eyes glinting with excitement. "Actually, I'm thinking of applying for admission to Riverside University."

Zane raised an eyebrow, surprised. "Oh, really? That's where I'm attending."

Her lips curved into a playful smile. "Oh, really? I guess that works out then. I heard it's a great place, and I was already looking into it. I guess you could show me around if I end up getting in."

Zane chuckled, surprised by her confidence. "Well, I'd definitely be down to give you a tour if you come."

"Well, thank you," she replied with a warm smile. "I'll definitely keep that in mind." She looked at him with a spark of challenge in her eyes. "But maybe I'll be too busy making new friends to need a tour guide."

"I can be persuasive," Zane said with a teasing grin. "Besides, once you're there, I'll make you my girlfriend."

Her eyes widened just a fraction before she laughed, the sound bright and unfiltered. "Oh, will you now?"

"Count on it," Zane shot back, the words leaving his lips before he could even stop them. His heart raced a little. Was he being too forward? But it felt right, like a natural progression of the moment.

She studied him for a moment, her gaze curious, a little amused. "You're bold, I'll give you that. But I'll hold you to it if I come."

"I'll be waiting," Zane said with a wink, not entirely sure if he was joking or if a part of him actually hoped she would take him seriously.

The rain continued to fall, a steady rhythm that seemed to echo the beat of Zane's heart. He didn't know then what the future would hold. He didn't know that it would be three long years before her name would light up his screen again, her message a spark that would reignite everything he felt in that fleeting moment by the waterfall. But as the day wore on, and the memory of her laugh stayed with him, he knew one thing with absolute certainty:

Some meetings are more than chance; they are stories waiting to be written.

And with that, Zane felt a spark of something more, something deep inside that whispered of possibilities and what-ifs, a lingering connection that he didn't yet understand but would one day come to know. The day was winding down, but something about her felt like the beginning of something new.

As the group made their way back to the car, Zane couldn't help but steal a few more glances at her, now fading into the crowd. The thought of her lingered in his mind, mixing with the sound of rushing water and the soft hum of distant voices. He didn't know what the future held, but he couldn't shake the feeling that, somehow, he had just met someone who might change his life.

CHAPTER TWO

FRAGMENTS OF A HEART

As a child, Zane was a small, chubby boy, his frame an easy target for ridicule. His classmates, quick to pass judgment, seized every chance to mock him, crafting cruel nicknames that stuck to him like a second skin. Their laughter wasn't just noise; it carved itself into him, leaving invisible scars he carried long after the jokes had ended. Even the teachers, the ones he had hoped might notice his quiet battles, seemed blind to his pain. Instead of offering a hand, there were only sharp words and dismissive glances. To them, Zane was a troublemaker, a boy too restless and too mischievous to be worth the effort.

But underneath it all, Zane wasn't seeking chaos. He was seeking a connection. Every outburst, every reckless joke, every clumsy attempt to join a conversation was just a hand stretched out, hoping someone would take it. Yet time and time again, he was met with rejection. Friends laughed behind his back. Girls looked through him as if he weren't even there. Every snicker, every cold glance chipped away at him, until eventually he learned it was safer not to reach out at all.

Over time, Zane built walls around himself. Not because he wanted to shut the world out, but because the world had made it clear he wasn't welcome in it. Behind those walls, a lonely boy sat, wishing more than anything that someone would see past the noise, past the labels, and simply understand him.

The isolation grew heavier with each passing year. Even though he longed to be accepted, the weight of public humiliation pressed down on him without mercy. It wasn't just the schoolyard jokes that wounded him. It was the private shame, the quiet understanding that no one truly knew him.

When the darkness of isolation became unbearable, Zane found himself standing at the edge of an abyss. One day, overwhelmed by the pain, he even held a blade in his hand, wondering if it would be easier to just disappear.

It was a fleeting thought.

The image of his parents, broken and devastated, stopped him. They needed him more than he could bear to hurt them. That small hesitation, that tiny moment of choosing to stay, marked something important inside Zane—a spark of resilience he didn't even know he had.

One evening, as rain tapped gently on the windows, Zane sat across from his mother at the kitchen table. She looked up from chopping vegetables and said softly,

"You've been quiet lately. Not the usual Zane."

He hesitated, then shrugged.

"Just tired," he said. But then, almost in a whisper, he added, "Do you think I'm a failure?"

She stopped, wiped her hands, and sat beside him.

"Zane, your scars make you strong. But your heart? That

makes you unstoppable. I see you. Always have."
It wasn't a dramatic moment. Just words. Simple and soft.
But they stayed with him.
As the years passed, he carried his burdens quietly. But underneath the surface, that flicker of hope refused to die.
In his later school years, he found a small circle of friends who appreciated his humor and quirks. They skipped classes together, laughed at the world, and for a little while, Zane forgot what it felt like to be alone. Still, even in the middle of those happy moments, an emptiness lingered. A feeling that no matter how much he laughed, he was still drifting without a real purpose.
One late night on the hostel rooftop, his friend Jay passed him a bottle of soda and said,
"You know, man, I used to think you were just the funny guy. But you've got depth, Zane. Real depth."
Zane chuckled awkwardly.
"Yeah, well... people usually just see the fat kid who can't shut up."
Jay frowned.
"Screw that. I see someone who survived. Who's still fighting? And that's more badass than anything."
And for the first time in years, Zane felt... seen.
Then came another blow. When it was time for college admissions, he was rejected from the prestigious college he had dreamed of. The sting was sharp and bitter, confirming what he had always feared deep down, that he wasn't enough.
But sometimes life opens a door just when you think all of them are closed.
One afternoon, while aimlessly scrolling through videos on his phone, a thumbnail caught his eye — "Bringing Fantasy Worlds to Life."

Curious, he clicked. What he saw blew him away: vivid digital landscapes, animated characters, entire universes made from scratch.

Zane sat up.

"People do this for a living?" he murmured.

That night, he stayed up till 4 a.m. watching tutorials, sketching rough characters in an old notebook, heart pounding with a strange, thrilling certainty that this was what he was meant to do.

By pure chance, he had stumbled upon the world of game art and development. The idea of creating worlds and breathing life into stories lit a fire in him that he had never felt before. He threw himself into learning everything he could, balancing it with his college studies, fighting every day to build a future he could believe in.

College didn't become a place of rejection anymore. It became a place of transformation. Slowly, piece by piece, he began to reinvent himself, shedding the limitations of the boy he used to be.

He started spending more time with his family. Spending time. Talking. Listening. Laughing. They, too, saw the change in him, not just in what he did, but in how he looked at the world. With a quiet strength that hadn't been there before.

His days started filling up with sketching between classes, helping juniors, and talking more openly with friends. But still, something was missing. A sense of still being incomplete.

He often wondered, "Maybe I've rebuilt myself... but do I know who I'm rebuilding for?"

He had no idea that the answer to that question would walk into his life the very next semester, with eyes like oceans, and a voice that sounded like home.

CHAPTER THREE

AVA AND ZANE

Her name was Ava.

At first, Ava was just another face in the crowd, warm, full of life, the kind of person who naturally drew others in. Something about her made even the heaviest rooms feel lighter, like she carried a bit of sunshine wherever she went. Her laughter was effortless, her spirit fierce, and she wore her kindness like a second skin.

But as time passed, she became more than just another bright face in a world that often felt too cold. She became Zane's rock.

While others remained absorbed in their worlds, Ava noticed him. Really noticed him.

"You always sit here after class," she said once, sitting beside him on the quiet bench near the art building.

"It's peaceful," Zane replied, avoiding her eyes.

"Or lonely?" she asked gently.

He shrugged, a small smile tugging at his lips. "Maybe both."

That was how it began casually, like two strangers sharing the same silence. But it didn't stay that way for long. They started talking about school, about life, about the small, stupid things that somehow made the hardest

days easier.
"Do you think sloths know how slow they are?" Ava once asked in the middle of a deep conversation about time.
Zane laughed, surprised. "I don't know... but if they don't, that's kind of beautiful."
"Exactly," she grinned. "Maybe we don't need to rush either."
Those casual conversations turned into late-night talks, the kind that stretched until the sky turned pale.
"I don't show people my sketches," he confessed once during a 2 a.m. phone call.
"Why not?" she asked.
"They never feel good enough."
"Zane," she whispered, "they don't have to be perfect to matter. You don't have to be perfect to matter."
Zane found himself opening up in ways he never thought he could. He shared his dreams, his fears, the parts of himself he usually kept hidden behind jokes and sarcasm. And Ava didn't flinch. She listened. She understood.
"I used to hate mirrors," he told her one day. "Because all I saw was someone who didn't belong."
"Then I'll be your mirror," Ava said. "Because I see someone strong. Someone who matters."
Through Ava, Zane experienced something rare: kindness without conditions. She made him realize he didn't have to hide behind walls or wear masks to be liked. He could simply be.
He laughed more around her real, unfiltered laughter, the kind he had almost forgotten he was capable of. He started believing in good days again. In possibilities. In himself.

Ava was the reason Zane's art improved. Before she entered his life, he never believed his creations were worth showing.

"You drew this?" she asked one day, picking up a sketch from his notebook.

He reached out to grab it back. "It's nothing."

"Zane, it's you. And it's beautiful."

That simple statement stayed with him for days.

With her quiet encouragement, he began to see the value in his work, not through validation, but through the sincerity in her eyes every time she looked at it. So, Zane poured more of himself into his pieces. His art became his voice, and Ava, unknowingly, became his muse.

She was also the reason Zane began to connect with his parents in a way he never had before.

"Do you ever talk to them?" Ava asked once after Zane told her about keeping things from his family.

"Not really," he admitted. "They don't get it."

"They won't if you don't let them try," she said softly. "Sometimes love is just... waiting for the door to open."

Her words stuck. Eventually, he began letting his parents in, sharing small pieces of his world with them. And with time, they responded. For the first time, his house felt less like a place he lived in and more like a home.

Ava also helped him trust people again. Slowly, carefully.

"You're always watching the exits in a room," she said once.

"Habit," he replied.

"Maybe try watching the entrances. You might be surprised who walks in."

Because of Ava, Zane started believing that not everyone was out to hurt him. Her faith in people was contagious. He started talking to classmates, initiating conversations, even letting people see the real him, the boy behind the scars and the silence.

And perhaps most importantly, because of Ava, Zane began to believe that he was enough.

"What if I never become who I want to be?"

"Then I'll still be proud of who you are," she said, without hesitation.

"Why?"

"Because even your worst day is still worthy of love."

Ava was the kindest, most intelligent, and beautiful person Zane had ever known. Her presence had a quiet power; she didn't need to raise her voice to be heard. Her words were like melodies, and her eyes were like oceans deep, mysterious, and comforting all at once.

Zane had never been the kind of person to fit in at college, but because of Ava, he found himself showing up every day, hoping to catch a glimpse of her.

"You know I come to class just to see you, right?"

Ava smirked. "Oh, I know. I just pretend not to, so you'll keep trying."

"You're evil."

"I'm your kind of evil," she teased, nudging his shoulder. Everyone seemed to want a piece of her light, but Zane was content just to be near her. Even if he didn't say everything he felt, he knew it was real.

Ava was a soul that made Zane feel human again. In a world that had often made him feel invisible, she pulled him back in, reminding him that there was beauty in being seen, in being loved, in simply being.

She was the reason he smiled without pretending. The reason he dared to dream again. The reason he became the man he had always hoped to be.

CHAPTER FOUR

JUST ZANE

The realization hit him like a wave, and it terrified him. Zane had spent years building walls around his heart, each one crafted with care and caution. They were strong, he thought they would never fall. But Ava? She made him question everything. She made him wonder if it was time to tear them down. The feelings he had for her weren't just the usual friendly affection; they were deeper, stronger, and more real than anything he'd felt in years. And that thought scared him. How could he admit it? What if it ruined everything? What if he lost her? After all, Ava wasn't just anyone; she was his only true friend in a world that had often been cold and unkind to him.

So, Zane tried to bury it. He pushed his feelings deep down, telling himself that it was better to be silent than risk everything. But no matter how hard he tried to suppress it, the feelings grew. Every laugh they shared, every late-night conversation, just made it worse. It all felt so natural between them, like maybe just maybe there was something more. He longed to tell her, to confess what was building inside of him, but the fear of rejection was too great. The thought of losing her as a friend, of losing her altogether, kept him quiet. He convinced himself that if he just kept supporting her, just kept being there for her, maybe one day she'd see how much he cared. Maybe, just maybe, she'd feel the same.

Ava, for her part, seemed to notice the shift. There were moments fleeting, but real, when their eyes would meet, when their laughter would linger a little longer than usual, and Zane would feel a flicker of hope. Maybe, just maybe, she felt it too. But those moments were always brief, fading before he could truly understand them. And as time passed, Zane realized that maybe he was just fooling himself. Maybe the love he hoped for wasn't meant for him after all. Maybe he wasn't meant to have the kind of love he'd always dreamed of.

One evening, under a soft orange sky, they sat side by side on the old stone bench in the college courtyard. The air smelled faintly of rain, and a breeze played with Ava's hair as she looked up at the clouds.

Ava:

"Don't you ever wish life were simpler? Like... no mixed signals, no guessing games. Just clarity."

Zane paused. He wanted to tell her that she was the confusion and the clarity all at once.

Zane:

"Yeah. I think about that a lot. But maybe if it were simpler, we wouldn't feel things this deeply either."

Ava looked at him, surprised.

Ava:

"You're deeper than you look, Zane."

Zane smiled faintly.

Zane:

"You make me that way."

There was a long silence between them, not awkward, just full of things unsaid.

A few days later, after a long walk, they stopped at a small tea stall near the lake. The soft hum of crickets filled the background.

Ava:

"You're always there for me, you know? Sometimes I don't even know why you care so much."

Zane (without hesitation):

"Because you matter. That's all."

She looked at him, then really looked, and Zane saw something flicker in her eyes. Guilt? Confusion? Affection? He couldn't tell. But she looked away too quickly, sipping her tea to avoid his gaze.

That night, the silence of his room pressed in as he stared at their chat.

Zane (texting):

"Ever think about what we'd be like if we weren't... just friends?"

A long pause. She was typing. Then not. Typing again.

Ava:

"Sometimes. But... it scares me."

Zane:

"Me too. But not as much as the idea of losing you."

She left it on read.

Later, during a phone call, her voice sounded distant, not because of the signal, but something deeper.

Zane:

"You've been quiet lately. Everything okay?"

Ava (softly):

"Yeah, just... life. I've been thinking about a lot of stuff. Trying to figure myself out."

Zane:

"Am I part of that stuff you're thinking about?"

She paused.

Ava:
"That's the problem, Zane. You're too much a part of it."
The line went quiet again. And so did his heart.
Then came the turning point, the moment that changed everything.
Days turned into weeks. Conversations became shorter. Zane began to sense something changing, not just in Ava's tone or the way her replies came hours late, but in the way she started talking about someone else more often. A new name kept slipping into their conversations. At first casually, then more frequently, like a song stuck on repeat.
"He said this funny thing today,"
"He helped me with a project."
"He's just always there when I need to talk."
Zane tried not to overthink it. But every mention of this guy made his stomach tighten. He smiled through it. Laughed with her. Told himself it was just a friend, just like him.
But one evening, it became real.
It was late afternoon. Zane had stayed behind after class to meet a friend, but decided to take a longer route back through campus. As he passed the small courtyard their courtyard he saw her.
Ava.
She was sitting on the grass, barefoot, laughing.
And beside her, the guy.
He wasn't holding her hand, but their bodies leaned into each other as if gravity had chosen to bend around their connection. She smiled at him the way Zane once dreamed she'd smile at him. He watched the guy tuck a strand of hair behind her ear, and she didn't flinch. She let him.
Zane froze.

Something deep inside him cracked—not with the violence of a shatter, but with the slow, aching snap of something breaking quietly under too much pressure.

He turned before they could see him. Walked away. Fast. Eyes stinging. Chest tight.

That night, Zane couldn't sleep. He scrolled through old messages, their inside jokes, their late-night conversations. Everything that had felt like something now felt like a lie.

And yet... he needed to know.

The next day, he met Ava like nothing had changed. She greeted him with that same warm smile. And it almost made him hate her, how easy it was for her to be normal when he was falling apart inside.

They talked, walked, and eventually sat under the same old tree they always did.

And then he asked, as casually as he could:

Zane:

"So... that guy. The one I saw you with yesterday. What is he to you?"

Ava's smile faded slightly. She looked down at her hands, then back up at him.

Ava:

"He's... someone I care about."

Zane swallowed hard.

Zane:

"Care about... how?"

A long pause. Her voice was barely a whisper.

Ava:

"He's the person I love."

It was a single sentence, but it hit Zane like a punch to the gut. His breath caught. The world seemed to tilt. He wanted to scream, cry, laugh, say something cruel, but he didn't. He just nodded.

Zane:

"That's... that's great, Ava. I'm happy for you."

It was the biggest lie he'd ever told.

Inside, something in him crumbled completely. He had spent so long building hope quietly, nurturing feelings in silence, giving all of himself in the shadows, only to find that someone else had already taken the place he had dreamed of.

That night, Zane sat alone on his rooftop, staring at the stars they used to talk about. The sky looked the same, but everything else had changed.

He didn't cry. Not yet. He just sat with the weight of it all. The ache. The finality.

He had loved her. And she had chosen someone else.

And maybe that was the most painful kind of heartbreak, not being betrayed, not being forgotten—but simply... being unseen.

CHAPTER FIVE

AFTER THE STORM

After everything that had happened with Ava, Zane was left feeling like a shell of the person he once was. The weight of heartbreak, the constant barrage of self-doubt, and the endless questions about how he had let himself get so lost in it all? For weeks, he wandered in the fog of confusion. The bitterness, frustration, and anger swirled inside him like a storm that never seemed to quiet. He blamed himself, feeling as though he'd failed, letting emotions dictate his every decision. He had let himself believe in something that was never meant to be, and now he was left to pick up the pieces of his shattered heart.

The more he thought about it, the more questions haunted him. What if he'd done something differently? What if he'd seen the signs? But, in the end, none of those questions led to any answers. They only deepened the wounds.

For two months, Zane locked himself away. He stayed in his room, surrounded by the silence, hiding from the world as though that would somehow protect him from the pain. He convinced himself it was what he needed—time to heal, to reflect, to figure things out. But in truth, it was just a way to avoid confronting the mess he had made of his life. Every day was a cycle of pretending everything was fine while the weight of his unresolved grief pressed on him like a thousand pounds.

He told himself he was fine. He told himself that the isolation was helping him move on. But as time passed, the walls he'd built around himself grew higher and higher. The silence wasn't peaceful anymore, it was suffocating. The more he shut the world out, the more trapped he felt. He was stuck in his own mind, cycling through anger, regret, and sadness, unable to escape.

Then, one day, reality hit him like a slap across the face. His family was struggling. His father had racked up significant debt, and his brother wasn't in a position to help. They were barely making ends meet. Zane could no longer ignore the responsibility that weighed on his shoulders. He wasn't a kid anymore. He was the man of the house now, and his family was counting on him.

Zane stood at a crossroads. Was he really going to let his past, his mistakes, his heartbreak dictate his future? Was he going to let a failed relationship define him for the rest of his life?

No. He couldn't. His family needed him. He needed to find a way out of this emotional labyrinth. Would spending his life wallowing in self-pity over Ava's rejection help anyone? He knew the answer.

So, with one last look at the mess he'd made of himself, Zane made a decision. He was done. It was time to step up.

But moving on wasn't as easy as just deciding to. It required action. And that's when something deep inside him shifted. A part of him that had been dormant for too long stirred awake. He didn't want to be the broken version of himself anymore. He wanted to move forward. He wanted to be someone.

He threw himself into his passion for game art. He had discovered it during his college years, and it had always intrigued him. Now, it felt like the perfect way to escape the storm in his head. He immersed himself in research, learning new techniques and pushing himself to improve.

He applied for jobs, networked with industry professionals, and sent out portfolios with the hope that someone, somewhere, would give him a chance.

There were times when it felt like a losing battle. The doubts crept in. What if this doesn't work out? What if I'm not good enough? But Zane kept pushing through. He couldn't afford to give up. His family was depending on him, and the thought of letting them down was enough to fuel his determination.

Finally, after what seemed like an eternity, the hard work began to pay off. Zane landed a remote job during the COVID pandemic, just what he needed. The pay wasn't extravagant, but it was enough to support his family. For the first time in years, Zane felt like he was back on track, like he had control of his life again.

He wasn't looking for validation from anyone. He had built this life with his own two hands, and it felt like an accomplishment he could finally be proud of.

Still, even in the calm, there was a restlessness inside him. There were moments when the silence of his life felt heavy, like there was something missing. He was content, yes, but he couldn't shake the feeling that there was more to life than this. What did the future hold for him? The uncertainty gnawed at him, but he pushed it aside, focusing on his work and his family.

And then, one day, everything changed.

A few of his old friends, the ones from school, suggested a spontaneous trip to a waterfall. They were looking for something simple, a break from the routines of life. Zane agreed to go, needing the distraction. The trip wasn't supposed to be anything special. Just a few friends, nature, and a chance to unwind.

But when they reached the waterfall, something inside him clicked. As they hiked through the lush greenery, laughing and joking, Zane felt a calmness he hadn't experienced in years. The roar of the waterfall, the cool mist against his skin, it felt like a world away from his troubles. The beauty of the place reminded him of how much he'd grown, of how far he'd come from the angry, heartbroken kid he once was.

He stood at the edge of the water, lost in thought, letting the serenity wash over him. For the first time in a long time, he allowed himself to reflect not just on the pain, but on everything that had shaped him. He wasn't that kid anymore. He wasn't defined by his past mistakes. He was stronger now, more focused. And for the first time, he realized how much he had to offer.

And then, like a slow realization, he saw her.

She was standing at the edge of the water, her gaze distant, almost as if lost in the beauty of the place. Zane's attention was immediately drawn to her, though she didn't acknowledge him. There was something about her, something that made him look twice. It wasn't dramatic or over-the-top, but the way the sunlight hit her hair, the confidence in the way she carried herself it caught his eye.

He didn't know who she was, didn't know why she had such an effect on him. But in that brief moment, something shifted. Something about her presence lingered in his mind, and he couldn't explain why.

He didn't approach her. He didn't say anything. But as the day wore on, he found himself thinking about her, trying to piece together what it was that made him feel this way. Could it be fate, or was it just a fleeting moment? Little did Zane know that brief meeting by the waterfall was the start of something he couldn't yet understand.

CHAPTER SIX

CROSSROADS

A month had passed since the trip to the waterfall, but the memory still lingered in Zane's mind like a vivid dream. That moment, the girl standing near the water, her eyes distant, the light catching her features it had carved itself into his thoughts more than he cared to admit.

Zane had been back at college now, the sounds of the waterfall still echoing in his mind. The rush of the water, the cold spray against his skin, it all felt like a lifetime ago. He had been so sure of himself back then, but now, the familiarity of his college campus felt strange. Almost suffocating.

His friends had asked him about the trip, about the people he'd met, but Zane wasn't in the mood for small talk. He had come back to a life that still felt the same, but he didn't feel the same. His eyes weren't as focused as before, his mind wasn't as clear.

And then came the moment. The moment he'd been avoiding, the moment that had been sitting like a weight on his chest.

He saw her.

Ava stood across the courtyard, bathed in the soft light of the afternoon. Her brown eyes sparkled with the same warmth he remembered, and her smile was so familiar, so easy made Zane's heart skip a beat. But there was something different about her now, something he couldn't quite place. It was the way she held herself, the way her gaze lingered on him for just a second too long before she looked away, almost as if she wasn't sure how to react.

She was talking to someone else, but Zane knew that he couldn't just walk away. He had come back to a world that hadn't stopped moving, and neither had she.

Taking a deep breath, he made his way toward her, feeling the weight of the moment in every step. His heart pounded louder in his ears, and his palms felt clammy. Was this the right time? Would she even want to talk to him? He had no idea, but he couldn't turn back now.

Ava turned at the sound of his footsteps, her face lighting up when she saw him. That familiar smile. But this time, it didn't bring him the same comfort it once did. There was something else behind it, something distant.

Ava:

"Zane! It's been a while."

Her voice was warm, but there was an edge to it. Zane smiled back, but it felt forced.

Zane:

"Yeah. Been caught up with stuff."

He paused, unsure of what to say next. His eyes flicked briefly to the guy standing beside Ava, the one who had been with her when he had seen them together the other day. The guy didn't say anything, just nodded in Zane's direction, but the tension was palpable.

Ava's smile faltered for a split second, and Zane noticed it. He had always been good at reading people, and right now, Ava seemed caught between something between him and whatever this guy was to her.

Ava:
"How was your trip?"
Zane nodded, trying to keep his emotions in check.
Zane:
"It was good. Needed the break." He paused, glancing at her again. "How about you? How've you been?"
She looked away for a second, almost like she was thinking about how to answer. Zane's heart twisted. The distance between them was real now, more than just physical. He could feel it in the way she spoke, the way she avoided his eyes for a little too long.
Ava:
"I've been okay. Just... a lot going on, you know?" She let out a soft laugh, but it sounded more like a sigh. "College, life. It's all a bit much sometimes."
Zane nodded, unsure of what else to say. He wanted to reach out, wanted to ask if everything was really okay, but the words stuck in his throat. He wasn't sure where he stood anymore.
Before he could say anything, the guy beside Ava spoke up, breaking the silence.
Guy:
"Hey, we're gonna head to class. Catch you later, Ava."
Ava gave him a small smile and nodded before he walked away. Zane watched him go, his stomach twisting.
When they were alone, Zane took a step closer, his gaze falling to the ground. There was so much he wanted to say, so much he needed to say, but all of it felt too heavy to carry right now. Instead, he cleared his throat.
Zane:
"So, uh... You and him, huh?"
Ava stiffened slightly at the question. Her eyes darted to him, then away, her hand fidgeting with her bag strap.

Ava:

"Yeah. We've been hanging out a lot lately. He's a good friend."

Zane forced a smile, but it felt like it was breaking him apart inside.

Zane:

"Good friend, huh?"

Ava glanced at him again, a little too quickly this time. Zane saw the faintest flicker of guilt in her expression before it vanished.

Ava:

"Yeah. He's been there for me."

There it was. The final blow, wrapped up in a few simple words. She had found someone else. Zane had known it for a while, but hearing it from her lips made it real. And somehow, it hurt more than he'd ever imagined.

Zane:

"Well, I'm glad you have someone. That's... that's good, Ava."

It came out colder than he intended, but he couldn't help it. The pain was too raw, too fresh.

Ava tilted her head, studying him for a moment. Her voice softened.

Ava:

"Zane... I didn't mean for things to get weird between us. I just... It's been a lot, you know? I'm still figuring things out."

Zane felt a pang of hope, a glimmer of the person he used to know. He wanted to believe her, wanted to believe that maybe things could go back to how they were. But he couldn't shake the image of her with him, with someone else. And maybe that was the hardest part of all: the realization that no matter how much he cared for her, it wouldn't change anything.

Zane:

"It's okay, Ava. I get it."

He turned to leave, but before he could take another step, he heard her voice again, soft and hesitant.

Ava:

"Zane, wait."

He stopped, but didn't turn around.

Ava:

"Are you okay?"

The question was simple, but it hit him like a wave. He wanted to say yes, to tell her that he was fine. But the truth was, he wasn't. He hadn't been for a long time.

Zane:

"I'm okay. Just... figuring things out too."

With that, he walked away, his heart heavy, the weight of unspoken words between them growing with each step.

CHAPTER SEVEN

Echoes of the Heart

For the next three years, Zane poured himself into rebuilding his life, but the process was far from smooth. After the heartbreak with Ava, he'd promised himself that he would never again let emotions take control. The crushing weight of regret and endless questions gnawed at him. Why had he let himself get so lost in it all? How could he have been so naive? These thoughts had become like an incessant echo in his mind. But the decision was made that he had to move on. He had no choice.

At first, it wasn't easy. The early months of his new job, working from home during the COVID pandemic, were filled with frustration. The work was more demanding than he'd expected. The tasks piled up, deadlines loomed, and despite his best efforts, he struggled to keep up. The isolation of working from home didn't help. Instead of the social interactions he was used to in an office environment, he found himself staring at the same four walls, feeling more and more lost with each passing day.

He would wake up, get dressed, and sit at his desk, feeling as if he were drowning in a sea of tasks he couldn't quite conquer. He tried to find comfort in the quiet of his home, but it felt suffocating. Day after day, the weight of his responsibilities seemed to grow. The loneliness of being at home, combined with the growing frustration of not being where he wanted to be professionally it all became too much.

Yet, Zane had no choice but to press on. His family was in trouble. His father had accumulated a significant amount of debt, and Zane's brother, who had once seemed like a potential support system, wasn't in a position to help. The responsibility had fallen solely on Zane's shoulders. His father, once his source of strength, now needed Zane's help to keep the family afloat. The financial struggles added pressure to everything else, making Zane feel like he was on the verge of breaking.

Still, he refused to quit. He wasn't a kid anymore. Among the few people Zane kept close during those years was Jake, a friend he had known since school. Jake was everything Zane wasn't at the time: grounded, rational, and emotionally steady. While Zane tended to bottle up his pain and carry it alone, Jake was the one who quietly showed up, no matter how distant Zane became. He didn't push Zane to talk, but he was always there when Zane needed an anchor, even if Zane rarely admitted it.

Whether it was late-night calls when the stress of work became unbearable or casual hangouts just to remind Zane that he wasn't entirely alone in the world, Jake was one of the few constants in Zane's shifting life. He never judged, never pried, just listened, offered honest advice, and made sure Zane kept putting one foot in front of the other.

He threw himself into his work. There were moments of self-doubt when he questioned whether he had the skills or drive to make it. But Zane was relentless. Every night, after his daily tasks were done, he'd dive into learning—whether it was an online course, a tutorial, or a book on improving his game art skills. The more he learned, the more he realized how much he didn't know. And yet, he pressed on. It wasn't about the quick wins or instant gratification. He understood now that success would come in small, steady increments.

At times, the journey felt overwhelming. But with each milestone completing a course, mastering a new tool, and landing a project, he began to see the fruits of his labor. Slowly, but surely, his confidence started to rebuild. It wasn't perfect, and the doubts never truly disappeared, but Zane began to feel like he was on the right track. For the first time in years, he allowed himself to believe that he might be capable of more than just surviving. He might actually have a future.

However, even as Zane found success in his professional life, his personal life remained stagnant. He had shut down emotionally. After Ava's betrayal, he had sworn never to let anyone get too close again. The wounds from the past were too deep, and Zane couldn't risk feeling that vulnerable. He had built walls tall, impenetrable walls, and they weren't coming down.

Casual relationships became the norm. Dates would happen here and there, but none of them were serious. Zane couldn't afford to get emotionally invested in anyone. He wouldn't risk it. He focused entirely on his work, on his family, and on the future he was working so hard to build. Anything else felt like a distraction. Anything that might make him feel might make him care was something he couldn't afford.

But even in this numb, controlled existence, Zane found himself drawn to someone. Her name was Tiffany, and for a brief moment, she made him think that maybe, just maybe, he could trust again. She was funny, kind, and beautiful, and when they met, it felt effortless. For the first time in a long while, Zane allowed himself to feel something other than anger or pain. The connection between them was undeniable. She made him laugh, made him feel alive again. For a fleeting moment, Zane thought that perhaps his cynical view of love was wrong. Maybe this was the real thing.

But Tiffany walked away.

Not with honesty. Not with clarity. Just a gradual fading. Her messages grew fewer, her tone more distant, her eyes no longer held the same light when they spoke. Zane noticed it, but he didn't want to believe it. He gave her the benefit of the doubt, believing she needed space, time, and understanding.

What he didn't know was that, during that silence, someone else had quietly taken his place.

Not a stranger. A friend. Someone who had been around, someone Zane had trusted enough to let close. Someone who knew what Zane had gone through and still chose to cross that line.

When the truth came out, it didn't come with apologies. Zane had to piece it together, little changes, a shift in energy, mutual friends going quiet. When he confronted Tiffany, she didn't deny it. She admitted she had grown close to someone else. That she didn't know how to tell Zane that things had changed. She said he had been emotionally distant... that it made her feel alone.

Maybe that was true. Zane had built walls. He had scars. But what stung wasn't just that she left, it was how easily she let go. How she had once told him he made her feel safe and seen, and yet when things got difficult, she chose silence over honesty.

The friend never said a word. He disappeared from Zane's life without explanation, as if what happened didn't deserve one.

Tiffany wasn't cruel. She didn't cheat in the most literal sense. But she knew what was happening, and still let Zane believe everything was fine until it was already too late. She didn't break him with rage or betrayal, she left him with quiet disappointment, the kind that lingers longer.

And in the end, Zane didn't yell, didn't fight. He just stood there, heart bruised but face calm, realizing once again that trusting people came with a cost he could no longer afford.

That was the day Zane stopped believing in second chances.

The betrayal hit him like a hammer. The pain wasn't just in the act itself, it was in the realization that he had been foolish enough to trust again. He had let his guard down, even for a moment, and it had cost him. The hurt was deep, but what cut even more was the confirmation of his worst fear that he was unworthy of love, that no one could be trusted, and that he would always be the one left behind.

That moment marked the end of any hope Zane had of opening his heart again. He became even more closed off, more detached from the world around him. No one could hurt him if he didn't let them in. Zane buried himself in his work, in his career, and in his family. He doubled down on the goals he had set. The pain from the betrayal was real, but it was also a catalyst, a painful reminder that emotions were a liability. They made him weak. They made him vulnerable.

So, he shut them out.

Zane became numb. The years passed, and while his professional life flourished, his personal life remained nonexistent. He didn't need anyone. He didn't need love. He didn't need anything except stability. His career and his family were all he had now. And that was enough to get him by.

But deep down, Zane knew there was more to life than surviving. He had lost sight of it, had buried it under layers of pain and fear, but somewhere inside, there was a flicker, a reminder of who he used to be.

And then, one day, everything changed.

A spontaneous trip to a waterfall with his friends. It wasn't anything special. Just a way to break from the monotony. But when Zane stood at the edge of the waterfall, the sound of the water crashing against the rocks, the mist on his face, the beauty of the scene, it hit him. For the first time in a long while, he felt at peace. The weight of the world wasn't on his shoulders anymore. The silence and serenity of the waterfall gave him the space to think, to reflect on how far he'd come and what he had left to do.

And that's when he saw her.

She was standing by the water, distant and unaware of his gaze. Her presence was magnetic. It wasn't love at first sight, not exactly. But in that moment, something inside him stirred. Something unfamiliar. A shift. He couldn't explain why, but he knew there was something about her—something that felt important. She didn't notice him, didn't acknowledge him at all. But the moment lingered in his mind.

Her name, as he would later learn, was Hayley.

For the first time in years, Zane felt something stir deep inside him. It wasn't a flash of instant attraction or desire.

It was a quiet knowing that maybe, just maybe, this wasn't just a random encounter. That brief glance, however unremarkable it seemed, felt like the beginning of something new.

But what? He didn't know yet. All he knew was that something was changing.

CHAPTER EIGHT

UNEXPECTED RETURNS

Zane's phone buzzed again, pulling him from his thoughts. He glanced down at the screen, frowning at the message from an unfamiliar number.

"Hey, it's been a long time. I wonder if you still remember me."

He read the message twice, the words unfamiliar yet oddly nostalgic. His brow furrowed. He didn't recognize the number. He hesitated before typing:

"Sorry, who's this? I don't have your number saved."

The reply came almost instantly:

"It's Haley... Remember? The waterfall, three years ago. You told me you'd make me your girlfriend when I joined your college."

The words hit Zane like a wave, crashing through his calm. Memories from that rainy day at the waterfall flooded back. Her smile, her boldness, the flirtatious banter—he could still feel the excitement of their brief conversation. He felt his heart beat faster, a mix of confusion and intrigue swirling inside him.

"Haley... Wow. That's unexpected. What made you
reach out after all this time?"
He set the phone down for a second, half-expecting it
to buzz again. When it did, it was almost immediate:
"I had your number saved for a long time. Thought
about texting you so many times, but I wasn't sure if you
still used it. Then I found you on social media and figured
I'd take a chance. Lucky guess, huh?"
Zane smiled, leaning back in his chair, a mix of surprise
and amusement playing across his face. He ran a hand
through his hair, his mind racing.
"Yeah, lucky guess..." he thought, his fingers moving
over the screen.
"So, what made you finally send that message?"
The reply was quick, almost playful:
"Honestly? I couldn't resist. I saw your profile, and you
looked... different. Thought I'd see if you'd changed as
much as your pictures."
Zane's smirk grew wider. He leaned closer to the
screen, his thumb moving over the keyboard with a
familiar confidence.
"Different how? Handsome, I hope."
There was a pause. Then a laugh came through the
phone:
"Confident, huh? Let's just say I'm impressed. But I'm
still waiting to see if you can keep up with the guy I
remember."
Zane chuckled softly, feeling the playful spark between
them.
"You'll see, alright. But let's not make this about me.
What's been going on with you?"
He didn't have to wait long for her reply, which came
almost instantly:

"Oh, you know. Same old, same old... But my birthday's coming up."
Zane raised an eyebrow at the mention of her birthday. The playful banter was fun, but this felt different. He leaned in, his fingers typing quickly.
"Oh really? What are you expecting for your 'grown-up' birthday? No water balloons this time?"
Her response came quickly, with a playful tone that made Zane smile:
"Not this year. But who knows, maybe I'll send you an invite to my 'grown-up' party."
Zane grinned, already feeling the back-and-forth growing more comfortable.
"A party, huh? I'm intrigued. Maybe I'll bring a surprise, too. Just don't expect any cake fights."
The conversation flowed naturally, teasing and light, until Zane couldn't help but add:
"Same college, huh? I guess you're living the dream now," he typed, leaning back with a hint of mischief in his words.
"But hey, don't let the professors get any ideas about me. I'm sure they've moved on from their favorite troublemaker."
Haley's response came in a flurry:
"Haha, you really think they'd remember you after all this time? You were the one who never showed up to class!"
Zane laughed aloud at that.
"Hey, I was a busy guy, okay? Some of us had bigger plans than homework."
She teased him further,
"And what were those plans? Saving the world, one skipped class at a time?"

Zane smirked as he typed back:
"Maybe. Or maybe I was just working on something that would make everyone regret not paying attention to me back then."
Her reply was delayed for a moment, but when it came, it was playful but curious:
"Mysterious, huh? You always were the quiet type."
Zane paused before responding, remembering the quieter version of himself from back then, the one who kept to the shadows. He could feel the shift, how much he'd changed since then.
"Yeah, well, the quiet ones always have the best stories. What about you? Any exciting tales from your college life?"
Her reply came almost instantly, but with a playful edge:
"Not as exciting as yours, I bet."
Zane chuckled, not ready to reveal the layers beneath his exterior.
"I doubt it. But maybe we can swap stories over a drink sometime."
There was a brief silence before Haley responded, teasing:
"Not as exciting as yours, I bet."
Zane smiled at the screen, his fingers itching to continue.
"Not as exciting? I doubt it. But maybe we can swap stories over a drink sometime."
The playful back-and-forth continued for a few days, and soon Haley was dropping hints about her upcoming birthday celebration, which was fast approaching.
"So, my birthday's coming up. Got any plans to surprise me? Or are you just gonna keep me guessing?"

Zane, feeling the pressure to keep the playful energy flowing, typed:

"I don't know... surprise you? I thought I was the one who was supposed to be surprised," he typed, his fingers lingering on the screen before adding a wink emoji.

"But, I mean, I could make it special... if you think you deserve it."

Haley replied quickly, with a teasing tone that matched his own:

"Oh, I definitely deserve it. But I'm curious now... what exactly do you have in mind? A big birthday party with everyone from college? Or something more private, just the two of us?"

Zane let the question simmer for a moment, considering his response. He knew Haley was playful, but he wasn't about to back down.

"A private celebration, huh? Bold. I'll admit, the idea of spending your birthday with you does sound tempting..."

Her reply was swift, and he could almost hear the smile in her words:

"Well, if you're up for it, maybe I'll take you up on that offer. Who knows, maybe you'll surprise me in ways I didn't expect."

Zane smiled to himself.

"Guess I'll have to plan accordingly then, huh? Can't leave you disappointed."

Haley's response was a playful eye-roll emoji.

"We'll see about that. But I have to admit, I'm really curious now."

"Curiosity is a dangerous thing, but hey, it'll be worth it," Zane replied, tapping the send button with a grin.

As the days passed, the conversation became more comfortable, each message a subtle test of their growing connection. Haley's birthday came and went, and Zane, caught up in his own work and life commitments, found himself unable to make it to the celebration. Work, family obligations, and the constant weight of his own thoughts kept him from reaching out, but he found himself thinking about her more and more.

A few days after her birthday, Haley messaged him:

"Hey, so we're going to watch a movie this weekend, and I was wondering if you'd like to join us? Some of my friends will be there, but I thought it could be fun if you came along."

Zane's fingers hovered over the screen, already feeling the familiar pull of her words, even though they were casual.

"A movie, huh? Sounds like a good way to catch up... if you promise not to make fun of my movie choices."

Haley responded almost immediately:

"Deal! I'll even let you pick the movie. But only if you promise not to choose some weird horror film."

Zane smirked, already feeling the playful energy between them.

"Hmm, no promises. But I'll try to keep it reasonable."

She responded with a laughing emoji:

"Alright, alright. Just show up and we'll see if we can actually enjoy the movie without you scaring everyone off."

He was already getting curious about the group she'd be with.

"Who else is coming with you? Don't tell me you're bringing a bunch of loud, rowdy friends."

Her teasing reply came quickly:

**"I'll be the judge of that, but don't worry, everyone's chill

CHAPTER NINE

THE SPACE BETWEEN US

Zane arrived at the theater, feeling the usual mix of excitement and uncertainty. The night was cool, the kind of evening that always felt perfect for something spontaneous. His hands were tucked in his jacket pockets as he scanned the crowd, eyes moving quickly until they landed on her.

There she was, Haley. Standing with a few friends, laughing. The marquee lights overhead cast a golden glow on her face, making her look almost unreal. She looked just like he remembered, bright brown eyes, wavy hair falling loosely over her shoulders, but there was something else now. A maturity, maybe. A distance. Or perhaps it was just the time they'd lost.

As he walked up, the nerves in his chest twisted and coiled. But then, her eyes met his, and just like that, she smiled.

"Look who finally showed up!" she teased, stepping forward and nudging his arm lightly.

Zane grinned, the tension loosening its grip. "Told you I'd come," he said. "Had to make sure I didn't miss out on

all the fun."
"You're late, by the way," she said, smirking.
"Fashionably," he added, cocking an eyebrow.
Haley laughed, just like before. "Alright, fair enough. Come on, we've got seats."
Inside the theater, they found spots with her group. Zane sat beside her, trying to play it cool, but a small part of him was acutely aware of the space between them and how close it suddenly felt.
The movie wasn't groundbreaking. In fact, halfway through, Haley leaned in and whispered, "Okay, I'll admit it. I picked a bad one."
Zane smirked. "Told you your taste was questionable."
"Oh please, Mr. 'I-watch-obscure-anime-in-black-and-white'," she retorted, bumping her shoulder against his.
He chuckled. "Touché."
When the credits finally rolled, the lights rose, and the crowd stirred around them, Haley turned to him, eyes sparkling. "So? Not too bad for a movie night, huh?"
"I mean... could've used fewer awkward slow-motion shots," Zane said with mock seriousness.
"I swear, you're impossible," she replied, laughing as they walked out into the night.
He paused. "Coffee?"
Haley nodded. "Yeah. We should talk."
They found a quiet café just around the corner. It wasn't crowded, just a few students typing away on laptops and a couple lost in conversation. They chose a cozy booth near the back.
Zane ordered a black coffee; Haley went for a caramel macchiato. As the drinks arrived, they settled in, the air between them soft and warm. For a moment, neither of

them spoke.

"So..." she started, stirring her drink slowly. "How's life?"

Zane took a sip before answering. "Busy. Grounded. I've been working a lot. Trying to keep things moving for the family. For myself."

Haley tilted her head. "You've changed. I mean, you seem more... calm. Collected."

Zane gave a soft shrug. "Had to grow up a little. Life didn't really give me a choice."

She nodded. "Yeah. I get that."

There was a silence, comfortable at first, then heavier.

"What about you?" he asked. "How's life treating you?"

Haley looked down at her drink. "It's been... weird. College was good, in parts. But... relationships, family stuff... I don't know. I guess I've been figuring myself out."

He nodded, genuinely interested. "You always seemed like you had it all figured out."

Haley gave a soft, sad laugh. "That's the thing. I was pretending."

Zane leaned forward, resting his elbows on the table. "Pretending for whom?"

She hesitated. "Everyone. Even I, sometimes."

There was a long pause. Her fingers curled around the cup, her shoulders just slightly tensed. Then she looked up and met his eyes.

"Zane, there's something I've been meaning to tell you."

He felt a sudden chill. "What is it?"

"I'm in a relationship now."

The words hit like cold water. Zane blinked, the smile on his face fading for a heartbeat before he could recover.

"Oh," he said, managing a small nod. "I didn't know."

"I wasn't sure if I should bring it up," she said quickly. "I didn't want to ruin the night."

"No, no, it's fine," Zane said, voice even, almost too even. "You should've told me. I mean... I appreciate the honesty."

"He's... nice," she added, almost awkwardly. "Just... not everything's perfect."

Zane studied her for a moment. "Does he know you're here? With me?"

Haley looked away. "Not exactly."

"Right."

Another silence. This one wasn't so comfortable.

"I didn't come here with bad intentions," she said. "I just... I missed you, Zane."

His throat tightened. "You missed me, or you missed how I made you feel?"

Haley's eyes flicked up, surprised.

"I'm not accusing you," Zane said gently. "I just want to understand. We've both changed. But the truth is... I didn't expect this to feel so familiar."

She gave him a soft, broken smile. "Neither did I."

Zane ran a hand through his hair. "So what are we doing then? Sitting here, in this café, pretending like this doesn't feel like something more?"

Haley hesitated. "I don't know. I wish I had an answer."

He nodded slowly, finishing his drink. "Well... I guess sometimes, there aren't answers."

"I still want us to be in each other's lives," she said, her voice small.

Zane looked at her, his eyes searching. "I don't know if I can do halfway, Haley."

Her eyes welled, just a little, but she blinked it away. "I understand."

The night had shifted. Something between them had cracked something that had once been wide open, then buried, and now half-uncovered again.

When they finally stood to leave, Zane offered a ride without even thinking. "Let me take you home."

On the bike, the silence felt heavier, like something neither of them could shake. When they reached her place, she climbed off slowly, turning to face him.

Haley lingered by the gate, her fingers brushing the strap of her bag nervously. The porch light behind her cast a soft halo around her silhouette. Zane sat on his bike, helmet resting on the handlebars, reluctant to ride away just yet.

She took a step closer. "Hey…" Her voice was almost lost in the breeze. "Are we okay?"

Zane looked up at her, and for a moment, he didn't know how to answer. The weight of the night—the laughter, the comfort, the sudden gut-punch of her confession pressed against his chest. He forced a smile, the same kind he'd worn back at the café.

"We're okay," he said eventually. "Just… adjusting."

Haley nodded, her brow furrowed. "I wasn't sure if I should've told you. Part of me thought maybe I should just pretend like nothing had changed. But that didn't feel right."

"I appreciate the honesty," Zane replied, his voice softer now. "Really. I'd rather hear it from you than find out later… or worse, feel like I imagined something that wasn't there."

She looked away for a moment, her gaze falling to the pavement. "There was something there," she said. "Three years ago, and… even now. I don't know what it means, but I'd be lying if I said I didn't feel anything."

Zane's breath caught in his throat. He stood up, walking his bike forward a few steps until he was standing directly in front of her.

"But you're with someone now," he said quietly.

Haley nodded. "I am. And it's not perfect. It's... complicated. I guess everything is."

Zane looked at her, eyes searching. "Then why reach out to me again? After all this time?"

"I didn't plan it," she admitted, her voice trembling slightly. "I saw your profile on social media one day and just... I don't know. I felt this pull. Like maybe talking to you again would remind me of a version of myself I've lost. Or maybe I missed you more than I thought."

Zane looked down, then back up at her, his voice low. "You did more than just remind me of something. You made it all come back. The excitement. The connection. Even the pain."

A moment of silence passed between them, heavy, electric, unspoken truths charging the air.

"I never wanted to hurt you," she whispered.

"I know," he said.

Then he let out a breath, rubbing the back of his neck. "But Haley... I don't think I can do this if I'm going to be just some emotional escape when things get hard. I've been through too much to let myself fall into that again."

Haley looked at him, eyes wide, vulnerable. "I get that. I really do. I don't want to be unfair to you. I just... I don't know where I stand with anyone right now. Not even myself."

Zane stepped back slightly, nodding. "Maybe that's something you need to figure out first."

She looked like she wanted to say more, but the words didn't come.

"I should go," he said, forcing a small smile. "It's late."

"Zane..." she started, her voice unsure.

"Yeah?"

"Thanks for tonight. For coming. For not walking away."

He gave her a long look. "I'm not walking away. But I might need to keep some distance... so I don't lose myself again."

She nodded slowly, understanding. "Goodnight, Zane."

He nodded back. "Goodnight, Haley."

As he rode off into the night, the wind rushing past him couldn't quite clear his mind. Her words echoed again and again, each one chipping at the walls he'd carefully rebuilt over the years. And as the city lights blurred behind him, Zane knew this wasn't over.

Not yet.

CHAPTER TEN

FALLING INTO YOU

After weeks of spending time together, Zane and Haley had slipped into a rhythm that felt both comfortable and electric. What started as casual meetings had slowly transformed into something deeper, something more meaningful. It was the kind of connection that didn't need constant words to validate it, the kind of bond that formed in shared glances, quiet silences, and long conversations that had no agenda. Zane found himself looking forward to every moment with her, whether it was a spontaneous coffee run or a quiet walk in the park. Their time together wasn't just a distraction anymore; it had become essential.

Zane had always been someone who kept his guard up, but with Haley, it felt different. She seemed to understand him without him needing to explain every detail, as if she could read the spaces between his words. And Haley, who had always carried an air of caution, found herself more at ease than she ever expected. With Zane, there were no expectations, no judgment, just a shared sense of being, of existing in a way that made the world feel a little less heavy.

There was an undeniable current running beneath their conversations, an undercurrent that neither of them dared acknowledge fully, but both felt in the smallest gestures—the lingering look, the subtle touch of a hand, the playful way they teased each other. It wasn't just friendship anymore. They both knew it, but neither wanted to rush it, at least not out loud.

One evening, after an impromptu trip to the lake, they walked along the water's edge, the last rays of the sun casting a soft glow over the rippling surface. The air was cool and crisp, but the warmth between them was undeniable. It had been a peaceful, almost perfect day. Yet, as they walked in silence, Zane could feel the tension building; something was about to change. He could sense it in the way Haley's steps slowed, in the way her gaze became more distant.

They stopped by a large rock near the water, the sky now a brilliant canvas of pinks and oranges. Haley stood still, gazing at the horizon, as if the sunset held some answer she couldn't quite find. Zane mirrored her stance, his heart beating faster, sensing the change in the air. Something was shifting between them, something too important to ignore.

After a long moment, Haley turned to face him, her expression thoughtful, hesitant even. Her eyes met his, and for a second, Zane felt as if time had slowed. There was a vulnerability there—a softness that hadn't been there before.

"You know," she began, her voice low and almost uncertain, "I didn't expect to feel this way. About you, I mean. But... I think I might have feelings for you."

The words hung in the air, delicate and raw, and Zane's chest tightened. He had thought about this, wondered about it, but hearing it from her felt like an anchor dropping into the deep. He hadn't expected it now, not like this. He hadn't expected her to lay her heart so bare. For a moment, the world seemed to hold its breath, and Zane's mind spun.

Haley continued, her voice quieter now, almost as if she were reassuring herself more than him. "I didn't want to complicate things. I didn't want to mess up what we have. But... I can't ignore it anymore."

Zane's heart beat a little faster as her words sank in. This wasn't just a confession, it was an opening, an invitation to something more. He stood there for a second, unsure of how to respond. His mind raced with memories of their time together, the way she had made him laugh, the way they had shared their thoughts and fears. It had been building, slowly but surely, and now here it was. He had to answer her, but the words felt heavier than he expected.

He stepped closer, closing the space between them just enough that the air felt charged with something unspoken. "I think I've felt it too," he said quietly, his voice steady but layered with emotion. He could feel her looking at him, waiting, and it made his heart ache with both excitement and fear. "I've been trying to figure it out for a while, and it's been confusing. But now... I can't ignore it either."

Haley's eyes softened at his words, her shoulders relaxing a little as if a weight had been lifted. She took a breath, glancing down for a moment as if grounding herself before speaking again. "I wasn't sure you felt the same way," she confessed, her voice trembling just slightly as her fingers brushed his hand. "But now... I'm glad you do."

Zane's chest tightened at her touch, and before he knew it, his hand found hers, fingers interlacing without thinking. The moment felt right, too right to question, too right to hesitate any longer. They stood there, their hands connected, their hearts beating in a rhythm that seemed to align with the world around them.

"You know," Zane said, his voice low, almost a whisper, "maybe we should take this slow. I don't want to rush anything, but... I don't want to back away from it either. Not now, not with you."

Haley smiled softly, a mixture of relief and nervous excitement in her eyes. "I don't want to either. I just... I don't want to hurt anyone, especially not him, but I can't keep pretending like nothing's happening between us. It feels too real."

Zane nodded, understanding more than she knew. He had never wanted to rush her into anything, but the connection between them had been undeniable for so long. It was time to face it, to see where it would lead. They didn't need all the answers right now; they only needed to be honest with each other.

For a long moment, they stayed there, lost in each other's presence. The sunset faded behind them, and the cool night air swirled around them, but neither of them felt cold. The distance that had once felt insurmountable between them now seemed like nothing at all.

Then, without thinking, Haley stepped closer, her face tilted upward. Zane's breath caught in his throat as she closed the space between them, her lips brushing his in a kiss that was soft at first, tentative, almost fragile, but it quickly deepened, fueled by the emotions they had both been holding back for so long. It wasn't rushed or forceful; it was just the simple release of everything that had been building between them.

Zane's hands found their way to her waist, pulling her closer, and for a moment, the world outside them faded into the background. It was just the two of them; nothing else seemed to matter.

The kiss was slow and tender, their hearts syncing with each gentle press of their lips. And when they finally pulled apart, they stood there, breathless, faces flushed, but there was a certain understanding between them. The words hadn't been needed; the kiss had said everything.

"I think... I've wanted that for a while," Haley whispered, her voice trembling as she looked up at him with soft, uncertain eyes.

Zane chuckled, a little breathless. "Yeah... me too," he admitted, his hands still resting lightly on her hips. "But this... this feels different. It feels right."

Haley smiled, her fingers tracing the line of his jaw as if committing the moment to memory. "I'm glad we finally figured it out."

As they walked back together, side by side, the world seemed a little more clear, a little more open. The future still loomed ahead of them, uncertain and full of questions, but for the first time in a long time, they were both ready to face it together.

"It's getting cold," Haley murmured, wrapping her arms around herself as they walked away from the lake. The warmth of their kiss still lingered, but the evening breeze was starting to bite.

Zane shrugged off his jacket and draped it over her shoulders. "You really should start checking the weather before dragging me on these spontaneous trips."

She gave him a playful nudge. "Oh, please, you live for this kind of chaos."

Zane grinned. "Maybe. But only when it involves you." He glanced sideways at her, his voice softer now. "You really caught me off guard back there... but in the best way."

Haley looked down, her fingers fidgeting with the hem of his jacket. "I was scared to say it. I didn't know if I should. But I'm tired of pretending I don't feel something when it's this obvious."

Zane nodded slowly. "You're brave, you know. Saying what you feel, even when it's messy." He paused. "I've spent so much of my life trying to stay numb. It's easier that way. But you make it hard to keep those walls up."

She smiled at him, her expression softening. "Good. Maybe you're not supposed to live behind walls."

They walked in silence for a few more steps before Haley spoke again, her voice barely above a whisper. "What happens now?"

Zane exhaled. "We take it slow. We figure it out. And we be honest with ourselves and with each other."

Haley looked up at him. "Even if it hurts?"

"Especially if it hurts," Zane said firmly. "I'd rather face the pain with you than pretend there's nothing real between us."

CHAPTER ELEVEN

WHERE WE BELONG

After the night they shared, Zane and Haley's connection blossomed in ways they hadn't expected. The spark between them grew stronger, an undeniable force that neither of them could ignore. Haley found herself thinking about him more and more, and slowly, she came to realize that the relationship she had been holding onto for so long wasn't what she truly wanted anymore. What she had with Zane was something different, something real and full of potential. She knew, deep down, that she couldn't keep denying the bond they shared.

She couldn't stop replaying the way Zane made her feel safe, understood, and seen for who she truly was. No one else had ever done that for her. There were moments when she wanted to tell him everything, but the words always caught in her throat. What would he think? Would he even care?

One evening, while they were talking late into the night, Haley realized that her feelings for Zane had deepened beyond what she could ignore. The distance between them that once felt comfortable now seemed suffocating, and she knew she had to make a choice. She couldn't keep pretending that she wasn't ready for more, not after everything they had shared.

After much contemplation, Haley made a difficult decision. She ended her current relationship, feeling the weight of it but knowing it was the right thing to do. The connection with Zane had shifted something inside her; it was no longer a passing moment, but something worth pursuing. She reached out to him with the hope that he might feel the same way.

"Zane," she said, her voice trembling slightly but steady with conviction, "I think it's time we made this official. I don't want to hold back anymore. We should give this thing we have a name, a real one. I'm ready to see where this can go. Are you?"

Zane's heart skipped a beat, but instead of the thrill of excitement, a flood of uncertainty filled him. He had wanted this moment for so long, but now that it was here, he felt a heavy weight settle on his shoulders. His past relationships had left deep emotional scars, scars that made him hesitant to fully open up to someone, to risk feeling vulnerable again. He cared for Haley deeply, but the idea of putting a label on what they had made him nervous. It wasn't just about the connection they shared, it was about trusting someone again after so much hurt. He took a deep breath before responding, his voice soft but firm.

"Haley, I do care about you... more than I've let myself admit. But I'm not ready to jump into something so serious just yet. I need time to process things. My past is still affecting how I approach relationships, and I can't rush it. Not yet. I'm just not sure I can open up fully... not yet."

The words hung between them, a quiet tension filling the space. Haley's eyes softened as she listened to him, understanding but still feeling a pang of disappointment. She had hoped for a different response, but she also understood the weight of his past.

"I get it, Zane," she said, her voice gentle, though a hint of sadness lingered in her tone. "I just want you to know that I'm here for you. Whenever you're ready, I'll be here."

The moment was heavy with both unspoken emotions and a silent agreement between them. They would continue, but things were far from clear. Despite the uncertainty, they continued to see each other, spending time together, talking late into the night, sharing pieces of themselves that they had kept hidden for so long. The bond between them deepened, but still, they didn't speak about what lay beneath the surface of their feelings, their insecurities, and what this connection really meant.

There were times when they couldn't resist the chemistry between them, moments when their hands would brush or their eyes would meet with a look that held all the things they hadn't said aloud. The air between them was charged with anticipation, yet neither of them would cross the line to label it as something more than what it was until one evening, after a long conversation where they both shared pieces of their pasts, they found themselves drawn together again. The kiss they shared was familiar, full of longing and desire, but still, neither of them spoke about what it meant for them. It was a beautiful, silent surrender to the emotions they couldn't name, and yet, neither was ready to confront the reality of it.

Haley, however, began to feel the strain of Zane's reluctance to define their relationship. She couldn't help but wonder if she was just a temporary presence in his life, a distraction from the deeper scars he carried. She knew his past was complicated, that trust didn't come easily for him. But there were moments, small ones, that made her question whether she would ever be enough to break down his walls.

And when she saw his old friends around, laughing and reminiscing with him, she couldn't help but feel a sense of insecurity creep in. She wasn't part of that past, not in the way they were. She wasn't the carefree, innocent person Zane had once been, so it made her wonder if she was just a shadow of that time in his life. Would she ever measure up? Or was she destined to be another fleeting chapter in Zane's history?

One evening, as they sat in the dimly lit corner of a café, the silence between them grew heavy. Haley could sense the tension but didn't know how to address it.

"So," Haley began, her fingers nervously tracing the rim of her cup, "I've been thinking. Maybe... maybe I'm just not enough for you. Maybe this is just something temporary for you, something you're not really invested in."

Zane's eyes shot up, surprised at the sudden change in her tone. "What do you mean?" he asked, his voice tight with concern.

Haley took a deep breath, her gaze fixed on her cup. "I see the way you look at your friends when we're together. You laugh, you talk about the past... but I'm not a part of that. I never will be. And sometimes, I feel like I'm just filling a space for you, not really someone you're choosing to be with. Maybe I'm just not that person for you."

Zane's chest tightened, and for the first time, the words he had kept locked away spilled out. "Haley, that's not what this is. I don't know how to explain it... But it's not about you not being enough. It's about me, my past, the things that I carry with me. I'm scared, okay? I'm scared of opening up, of trusting again. It's not about you."

"I get that," Haley said, her voice soft but steady. "But I need to know if we're even moving in the same direction. I can't keep wondering if I'm just a placeholder in your life. I want to move forward, but I don't know how much longer I can keep waiting."

Zane's heart clenched at her words. "I'm not trying to make you wait. I care about you, Haley. I really do. I just... I need time. I need to figure things out. But I don't want to lose you."

She looked at him, searching his face for any sign of certainty. The vulnerability between them was palpable. "Then show me, Zane. Show me that you're in this with me. That you're not afraid to move forward."

Zane swallowed hard. This was the moment that would define everything. "I can't promise everything right now, but I can promise that I'll try. I want this, Haley. I do. I'll try... for you."

Haley nodded, a small, relieved smile tugging at her lips. "That's all I need, Zane. Just... try."

The moment was heavy, but it was also full of hope, a fragile hope that they could find their way to something real, despite all the uncertainties and fears. They didn't have all the answers, but they knew they were both willing to try.

In the days that followed, their connection continued to deepen, each moment of uncertainty slowly fading into a shared understanding. Neither of them had all the answers, but they were learning to trust in each other, step by step.

It wasn't long before their friends planned a trip to a secluded mountain. The place was quiet, far from the usual crowds, and the weather was misty, with the soft pitter-patter of rain adding to the peacefulness of the setting. It felt like the world had slowed down just for them, leaving Zane and Haley alone in their own little bubble. The moment was quiet, intimate, and full of possibilities. They wandered through the rain-drenched forest, their conversations flowing as naturally as the river beside them, but there was still an undeniable tension in the air.

At one point, Haley stopped walking, turning to face him. The rain had soaked her hair, and her eyes were soft, almost vulnerable. "I feel like we've been dancing around this for so long," she said, her voice quiet but filled with honesty. "I need to know if we're both ready for this. I want to be with you, Zane. But I can't keep waiting forever. I don't want to keep holding back."

Zane's heart raced in his chest, the vulnerability in her voice pulling him closer. He had been afraid of this moment, afraid to admit that he was feeling the same things. But standing there, with the rain around them and Haley so close, he knew it was time to face it.

"I know I'm not perfect," he said, his words soft but filled with sincerity. "But I want to try, Haley. I want to see where this goes with you. I just need a little more time to be sure."

Haley nodded, her expression softening as she understood the caution in his voice. She knew he had his reasons, his past, the scars that hadn't fully healed, but her heart ached with the desire to move forward.

"I get it," she said, her voice barely a whisper. "I just don't want to keep holding back anymore."

And then, without saying another word, they closed the gap between them. Their lips met in a kiss, tender and slow at first, but quickly deepening as they both let go of the tension that had been building between them for so long. It wasn't rushed, but it was full of the emotions they had kept buried for too long, the longing, the desire, the hope that this was the moment they had both been waiting for.

As they pulled away, breathless and content, they didn't need to say anything more. The rain continued to fall softly around them, and in that quiet, intimate moment, they understood each other perfectly. They didn't need to define everything; they just needed to be there with each other, allowing their connection to unfold at its own pace.

And so, they stood there, in the rain, unsure of what the future would bring but knowing, for that moment, that they were exactly where they needed to be. Together.

CHAPTER TWELVE

HAILEY

Haley's life had always been a delicate dance between light and dark, with moments of joy overshadowed by the lingering shadows of her past. She had spent years carefully constructing walls around her heart, hiding herself from the world, too afraid to let anyone see her true self. Standing at five feet tall, with bright, expressive brown eyes and wavy hair, she blended in well, never drawing attention to herself. But beneath her calm, unassuming exterior lay a vast ocean of emotions, untold stories, and unhealed wounds that few could ever hope to understand.

From a young age, Haley had been thrust into a world of pain and secrecy. As a child, she was a victim of abuse by her neighbors—an experience that marked her for life. She never found the courage to tell anyone what had happened, never spoke a word of it to her parents, friends, or anyone who could have helped. She carried that trauma in silence, forcing herself to ignore the pain and bury the memories. But no matter how hard she tried to move forward, the effects of those early years lingered, quietly shaping every aspect of who she became.

The weight of this secret grew heavy over time, and as she entered her teenage years, it began to affect her relationships. Her first serious relationship was a bittersweet reminder of how misunderstood she felt. Her boyfriend, though caring, was never able to truly understand her. He lacked the emotional maturity to see past her walls and the deep scars she carried. Instead of offering comfort and support, his lack of awareness created distance between them. He couldn't offer Haley what she needed, leaving her feeling isolated and abandoned. His immaturity wasn't just about age—it was about his inability to connect with her on a deeper emotional level. He couldn't see her struggles, and he didn't know how to be there for her in the way she needed. Eventually, the relationship dissolved, leaving Haley with a broken heart and a reinforced belief that no one could ever truly understand her. Her walls grew even higher, and she vowed never to let anyone close enough to hurt her again.

It was then that Zane came into her life.

Zane, with his steady presence and quiet strength, was different from anyone she had known. At first, Haley was unsure of him. He seemed to be a mystery to her—a person who wasn't easily swayed by the chaos around him. But there was something about him that felt safe. Zane didn't try to push her to talk about her past. He didn't expect her to open up immediately or try to fix everything. He simply gave her space, and in that space, Haley began to feel something she hadn't felt in years: freedom. With Zane, she didn't have to pretend. She could just be herself, no questions asked. And slowly, cautiously, she began to let go of some of the barriers she had built around her heart.

Yet, even as Haley opened up to Zane in ways she hadn't with anyone else, there was still a quiet battle inside her. She had learned to be independent and self-reliant, especially after her family's financial struggles had worsened. As the eldest child, she felt the weight of responsibility for her younger siblings. Her parents, though loving, were overwhelmed with their own burdens. And so Haley had stepped into a role she hadn't chosen but had to assume. The pressure was immense, and she often felt like she was drowning in a sea of expectations to be strong, to always be the one who held things together.

She had to be there for her family, no matter what.

But when Zane came into her life, it felt like an escape. For the first time in a long time, she could be vulnerable. Zane's understanding and patience made her feel safe enough to open up, but there was still something inside her that resisted fully letting go. Her past had taught her that trusting someone was risky. Every time she thought she was getting closer to letting herself feel fully for Zane, the fears from her past crept back in.

And then there were her friends. They didn't understand what she saw in Zane. To them, he was just another guy. Some of them even warned her against him, telling her that he wasn't good enough or that she could do better. Their words, though meant to protect her, only added to her confusion. Haley began to question herself. Was she making the right choice? Was Zane truly the person she needed, or was she just clinging to something that wasn't real?

Zane, however, remained steadfast. He could see the inner conflict in Haley. He noticed the way she would pull away at times, the way she struggled with trust and vulnerability. He wasn't blind to her hesitation, but he also knew something she hadn't fully acknowledged: she needed time. Zane had his own past—his own experiences that had shaped him into the man he was now. He had been through heartache and disappointment, and through it all, he had learned that love couldn't be rushed. He understood that Haley's fears ran deep, and he wasn't going to pressure her into anything. Instead, he gave her the time and space she needed, always there when she was ready, never forcing her to open up before she was comfortable.

But Zane's patience didn't mean he was unaffected by the situation. He had seen the cracks in Haley's walls, the way her past clung to her like a shadow, and he wanted to help. He knew that in order for their relationship to truly work, Haley needed to confront her past and heal. He was ready to support her in that journey, but he couldn't force her to take the first step.

As they spent more time together, Haley's confusion grew. She wanted to be with Zane, she truly did. But the doubts that plagued her every day made it hard to see a future with him. She was torn between the girl she had been—the one who had been hurt and betrayed—and the woman she was trying to become—the one who could embrace love and trust again. She needed to find a way to reconcile these two versions of herself, to heal the wounds that still bled beneath the surface.

One day, the inevitable conversation came. Haley asked Zane, "What do you want to do now? Do you want to make this official or not?"

Zane's heart skipped a beat. He had been waiting for this moment, but when it came, he wasn't sure how to answer. He had his own issues to work through. The weight of his past, his unresolved fears, and his own insecurities all came rushing to the surface. "I think I have some issues at the moment," he replied, his voice steady but filled with uncertainty. "I prefer not to talk about them right now."

Haley, looking at him with a mixture of understanding and sadness, took a deep breath. "Okay, Zane," she said softly. "This is the last message from me to you. I'm shifting to another city with my family. We're leaving this place, and this is the last time you'll hear from me. Don't call me again. Don't try to contact me again. This is goodbye."

The finality in her words hit Zane like a punch to the gut. He stood there, frozen, unsure of what to do or say. But in that moment, he realized something. Maybe, just maybe, they both needed to go their separate ways for a while. Maybe this distance would allow them both to heal, together or apart.

And so, their story came to a close, for now. The love they had shared, the connection they had built, remained in the hearts of both, but the future remained uncertain. As Haley moved on to the next chapter of her life, and Zane continued his own journey of self-discovery, they both carried with them the memories of what they had shared. And though their paths had diverged, the lessons they had learned from each other would remain, etched in their souls forever.

CHAPTER THIRTEEN

TANGLED HEARTS

As the days turned into months, and those months into six
or seven, Zane and Haley found themselves in an intricate
dance of closeness and distance. They were closer than
ever, sharing laughter, intimate conversations, quiet
moments that felt like the world had paused just for them,
but still, their bond remained undefined, unspoken. It was
a relationship in every sense except for one: it hadn't been
labeled. There were no promises made, no commitments
forged, no words of certainty. And though the chemistry
between them was undeniable, the absence of a label
lingered in the air, an unspoken tension neither of them
knew how to address.

Zane, deep in the recesses of his mind, was tangled in
his own emotions. The wounds from his past, the
betrayals, the heartbreaks, and the shattered trust were
still fresh, and they kept him from fully opening up. He
was afraid. Afraid of feeling too much, afraid of trusting
too fully, afraid of losing himself in something that could
slip through his fingers like sand. Each day, he felt his
emotions for Haley grow deeper and stronger. Every time
he saw her smile, or when she would reach out to him with
that familiar warmth, his heart would swell, but he kept it

buried. Zane wasn't sure what he wanted from her, or from this relationship. He knew he cared about her more than he had ever allowed himself to care about anyone in a long time, but the fear of getting hurt again kept him from embracing the truth of his feelings. He couldn't shake the thought that, maybe, he was just another temporary fix for Haley, someone filling a space until something better came along.

But in the silence of his mind, Zane's love for her continued to grow. Day by day, his feelings deepened. When she was around when she was near, the world seemed to shrink to just the two of them, and he couldn't help but be drawn to her. Her laughter, her touch, the way she cared about him in her own quiet way it all made him feel something he hadn't felt in years. Yet, he couldn't bring himself to admit it. He couldn't allow himself to be vulnerable, to let her see how much she meant to him. Instead, he kept his distance, fearing that once he gave in, once he allowed himself to fall completely, it would all slip away like it had before.

Haley, on the other hand, found herself caught in a whirlwind of emotions she didn't know how to navigate. She had given herself over to the connection they shared, but there was a part of her that felt adrift, uncertain of where she stood. She saw the affection in Zane's actions, the late-night messages, the small gestures of care, the way he listened when she spoke, the way his eyes softened when she was near but she couldn't decipher the silence that hung between them when it came to defining what they were. She didn't know if he was simply holding back out of fear or if he saw her as just another fleeting moment in his life.

Haley's uncertainty grew as the months went on. She tried to dismiss it, tried to focus on her own work, her college responsibilities, but the questions about Zane kept creeping in. What were they? Where was this going? Was he as invested as she was, or was she just another distraction? She knew she couldn't keep living in this limbo, and one evening, as they sat together after a long day, she couldn't hold it in any longer.

"I just want you to know, Zane," she said softly, her voice trembling ever so slightly, "I'm still here for you. Whatever this is, whatever you want to do, I'm here. I want you. I really do." Her words were a mix of love, longing, and vulnerability, and as she said them, a part of her braced for the possible rejection she hadn't been able to face before. She had always been open with him, but this time, there was a rawness in her voice that told him just how much she needed to hear the truth.

Zane's heart twisted in his chest at her words, but he could only offer a hesitant smile. On the outside, he seemed calm, collected, his usual self, but inside, his mind was spinning. He wanted to tell her everything, to let her know that he felt the same way, but he couldn't bring himself to say it. He wasn't ready to admit it, not when he wasn't sure if he could handle the vulnerability that came with fully committing.

"I don't know what I want right now, Haley," he said, his voice thick with hesitation. "I care about you more than I can say, but I'm not sure where we're going, or where I'm supposed to be. I'm still figuring things out." His words were a confession, a vulnerable admission that felt both like a relief and a burden. But as much as he wanted to open up, to let her in, he couldn't. Not yet. He wasn't sure he was strong enough to face the consequences of that level of commitment.

Haley nodded, her expression shifting from vulnerability to a quiet frustration. She had heard this before, and yet, something in her knew that this time, it felt different. Maybe it was the weariness in his voice, the way his words weren't as guarded as they had been in the past. But still, her heart ached. She had given him everything: her trust, her affection, her time,e and yet, it still wasn't enough. "I'm here, Zane," she repeated, the words heavy with emotion. "I'm here, and I'm not going anywhere. But I need you to decide what you want. I can't keep waiting, not like this."

The silence that followed was thick with unsaid words. Zane felt the weight of her plea, and for the first time, he felt a deep sadness in his chest. He knew he was pushing her away, but at the same time, he was holding on. He didn't know how to fix it, how to make it better, but he knew he couldn't keep living in this state of uncertainty. He had to make a choice. But what was he supposed to do when everything inside him told him to hold back, to protect himself, even though his heart longed to dive in, to finally let her in?

And so, they continued, caught in their own silences and doubts, yet still tethered by a bond that neither of them could quite explain. Zane, torn between his love for Haley and his fear of getting hurt again, stayed in the gray area, uncertain of where to go next. Every day, his feelings for her grew, but the question of commitment still loomed over him, and he wasn't ready to answer it. Not yet.

But as time passed, Haley's patience began to wear thin. She had been open, vulnerable, and honest with him, but the longer Zane held back, the more she began to question whether he was truly ready for the kind of love she was offering. She wasn't sure how much longer she could wait, but she also didn't want to give up on him. She had to decide whether her heart was worth the wait or if she needed to move on. And so, the unspoken tension between them remained, each of them silently waiting for the other to make the first move, while their hearts continued to grow more entwined with every passing day.

CHAPTER FOURTEEN

UNSPOKEN GOODBYES

The weeks leading up to Haley's final message were filled with a subtle shift in their relationship, one that neither Zane nor Haley fully understood at the time. What had once felt like an unspoken bond, where the connection seemed effortless, began to feel strained. It wasn't anything overt, no major fights, no harsh words, but the space between them started to widen, slowly at first, like a crack in an old window that no one noticed until it was too late.

Zane had always been cautious, holding back part of himself from Haley, guarding his emotions. He'd been hurt before, and the walls he built around his heart were meant to keep him safe. But with Haley, he had let those walls come down, inch by inch. At first, it felt good, liberating even, but over time, he began to notice the subtle signs of Haley pulling away. The late-night texts that used to be filled with laughter and flirtation turned into short replies, or sometimes no reply at all. Her calls became less frequent, and when they did talk, it felt like something was off, like they were both talking around their feelings rather than being open and honest.

Zane tried to brush it off at first. "She's just busy," he told himself, convincing himself it wasn't anything serious. But deep down, a small voice inside him kept whispering that something wasn't right. He noticed the change in the tone of her voice during their conversations, a faint shift in her words, as if she was no longer fully present with him, even when she was physically there. It made him anxious, uncertain. Was it something he had done? He had no answers, only a growing sense of discomfort.

Haley, too, felt the shift, but in a different way. Her life had always been a balancing act, filled with responsibilities, emotional weight, and unresolved questions about herself. But when she first met Zane, things seemed clearer. He was a source of comfort, someone who understood her more deeply than anyone ever had. Over time, though, doubts began creeping in, fed by the conversations she had with her friends. Their warnings started small at first, little things like, "Are you sure about him?" or "Do you know who he really is?" But the more they asked, the more she found herself questioning Zane, questioning everything they shared. Her insecurities flared up, fueled by her past trauma and the fear of getting too close to someone again.

Her family struggles didn't help either. She had always been the one to carry the weight of those around her, and it was starting to feel like too much. She felt herself withdrawing, not just from Zane, but from everyone. The very thing she had craved, closeness, understanding, was now the thing she feared the most. Every time she tried to open up, a little voice inside her warned, Don't let them in. Don't let them hurt you. And so, she shut down, pulling away from Zane without fully realizing what she was doing.

Zane noticed. The distance between them grew, like an invisible barrier that neither of them knew how to cross. The playful conversations that once filled their late nights turned into awkward silences, and Zane began to question if maybe it was all in his head. He tried to bridge the gap, texting her more frequently and calling her more often, but the responses were colder, more distant. He didn't want to force anything, but he couldn't shake the feeling that Haley was slipping away from him, and with each passing day, the ache in his chest grew.

He didn't know how to reach her anymore.

Haley, on the other hand, felt the pressure of her own internal struggle. What was happening between them? Was it just a phase, or was it something deeper? Every time she tried to think about their relationship, she became more confused. She still cared for Zane deeply. She enjoyed their moments together, but the weight of everything—the pressure to be perfect, the expectations of others, the trauma she hadn't healed from made it hard to truly connect. The more she tried to figure it out, the more overwhelmed she felt. She didn't know what to do or where to go.

Then came the night after their last real conversation. It was quiet, almost too quiet. Zane had sent her a text asking, "Are you okay?" It wasn't just about her well-being; it was a question born out of concern, out of a need to know what was going on. But Haley's reply was short, almost dismissive. "I'm fine. Just busy. I think we should take a break."

Zane stared at his phone, the words freezing him in place. A break? From what? From him? From everything? He wanted to ask, wanted to understand, but a part of him knew that no matter how much he tried to dissect her words, he wasn't going to find the answers. The air between them had shifted, and he felt the weight of it in his chest. She was pulling away, and no matter how much he cared for her, there was nothing he could do to stop it.

Days passed in silence. The once-constant flow of messages and calls came to a halt, and Zane began to retreat into himself. He couldn't bring himself to reach out again. It wasn't out of anger, but a sense of self-preservation. He had been through heartbreak before, and the idea of going through it again felt unbearable. The truth was clear, even if neither of them had spoken it aloud. They were drifting apart. And as painful as it was, Zane had to accept it.

Haley, too, felt the weight of the distance between them. Every day that passed without communication felt like a small wound that refused to heal. She wanted to reach out, but she couldn't find the words. She wanted to explain herself, to tell him why she had distanced herself, but fear held her back. Fear of being rejected, fear of facing her own truths. Every time she thought about contacting him, she hesitated. And with each passing day, the gulf between them widened.

Then came the message that neither of them could ignore. Haley typed the words, her fingers trembling on the screen. She knew it was the end, but it didn't make it any easier.

"Zane," she wrote, her heart racing in her chest, "this is the last message from me to you. I'm leaving this city with my family. Don't try to contact me again. Goodbye."

Zane's heart sank as he read the message, the words blurring in front of his eyes. He wanted to reach out, to beg her for an explanation, to tell her that he wasn't ready to let go. But deep down, he knew. Haley had made her decision. She was leaving, and there was nothing he could do to stop her.

The ache in Zane's chest was overwhelming. He stared at his phone, the reality of it sinking in. He wanted to scream, to fight for her, but the truth was clear sometimes, love just wasn't enough. The distance between them had become too great, and no amount of trying could bring them back together.

In that moment, Zane realized that sometimes, things just weren't meant to be. You couldn't force someone to stay, no matter how much you cared. You couldn't hold onto something that was already slipping away. And though it hurt deeply, painfully, it was a lesson he had to learn.

As Haley left the city, Zane was left to pick up the pieces of his broken heart. But this time, he knew he couldn't close himself off completely. He had learned the importance of connection, of love, and even of letting go. And as he stood there, letting the reality of it wash over him, Zane knew that he would heal eventually. It would take time, but he would heal.

Life went on for both of them.

CHAPTER FIFTEEN

THE QUIET HOPE

Months passed since Haley sent her farewell message, and though both Zane and Haley had begun the painful process of moving on, the echoes of their parting still lingered in the quiet corners of their minds. Each tried to carve out a new path for themselves, but the journey forward was not without its obstacles.

For Zane, work became a sanctuary. His career was growing steadily, and for the first time in a long while, he could feel the weight lifting off his shoulders. His days were filled with projects, meetings, and the constant hum of progress. The emotional numbness he had once wrapped around himself like a thick blanket was slowly melting away, revealing something new: a sense of purpose, a renewed desire to be more than just the guy hiding behind walls.

But even in the midst of the hustle, there were moments when Haley's face would appear in his thoughts, as if she were standing right beside him, as familiar as the passing breeze. He would catch himself thinking about her in the middle of his meetings or while sipping his coffee. Where was she? Was she happy? Had she found the peace she had been searching for? His fingers would hover over his phone, almost sending a message, but then he would stop. He remembered the goodbye, the finality of her words. No message ever came, but the longing for connection still simmered beneath the surface.

Zane had learned not to reach out, respecting the space she had asked for. He had come to understand that sometimes, relationships fade, not because of any grand reason, but because time and circumstances push people apart. It was painful, yes, but it was also a lesson in letting go of an essential part of life's journey.

Yet, in the quiet moments when the world slowed down, Zane would find himself staring at his phone, wondering what could have been. He accepted the truth that their lives were no longer intertwined, but that didn't stop the questions from swirling around. Would things have been different if they had both been ready? If life had been kinder? The possibilities haunted him for weeks, but as time passed, he began to understand something deeper. Sometimes, love and loss weren't meant to be answered; they were meant to teach you how to move forward, no matter how much it hurt.

For Haley, the fresh start in a new city had brought a semblance of freedom. The weight of her past was still there, lingering like an old scar, but she had learned to live with it. She had built a life for herself in this new place her own routine, new friends, and a sense of independence that felt both empowering and frightening. But there were days when Zane's absence was sharp. There were mornings when she would wake up with his face still imprinted in her mind, and nights when she missed the sound of his voice, the way he always knew what to say. She couldn't erase him from her thoughts, no matter how much she tried.

Her heart was caught in a tug-of-war between the past and the future, and sometimes, she couldn't help but wonder if she had made the right decision. She remembered the way they talked so easily, so effortlessly and how, for a time, it felt like they were two halves of a whole. But then there were moments of doubt, whispers from friends who didn't fully understand her connection to Zane. "Are you sure about him?" they had asked. "Is this really what you need right now?" Those words had lingered, growing louder with time.

She had tried to push those thoughts away, telling herself that she needed to focus on healing, on finding herself outside of any relationship. But every so often, the memories would surface. The way Zane made her laugh, the way he cared for her when she needed someone to lean on. She couldn't forget the way he had made her feel understood, as though she didn't have to hide behind walls anymore. And still, she couldn't shake the feeling that maybe, just maybe, their story wasn't finished.

What if? The question kept coming back, like a whisper in the dark.

But Haley was afraid. Afraid of what would happen if she reached out, if she opened herself up again. She had already walked away once, could she really go back? Could she face the uncertainty, the risk of getting hurt all over again? Or was it better to let the past remain where it was, locked away in memories?

It was the unspoken words that kept both of them tied together. The moments of silence stretched between them, thick with the weight of all that had been left unsaid. Zane kept himself busy, pushing away the longing and focusing on the things he could control. Yet, there were times when something reminded him of her, a song they had shared, a place they had visited together, or simply the way the rain would fall in the evening. It always brought him back to her, to the what-ifs.

Deep inside, Zane couldn't shake the belief that their paths would cross again someday. It wasn't just hope, it was something deeper, a quiet certainty that no matter how far they went, they would find each other once more.

Haley, too, couldn't escape the lingering connection. She would think about Zane late at night, when the world was still and her thoughts were free to wander. She knew she couldn't go back, not yet. But in her heart, she carried the possibility that maybe, one day, they would meet again. In a different place, at a different time. It wasn't something she expected to happen soon, but it was a quiet comfort, a thread that connected her to a version of herself that had felt deeply understood, deeply cared for.

And so, they lived their lives separately, but not without the quiet hope that their stories weren't completely finished. That somehow, somehow, they would cross paths again.

And when that day came, maybe they would be ready for each other. Maybe the timing would be different. But for now, they held onto that thought somewhere deep inside, both of them believed that someday, they would meet again.

Closing Thoughts

They had met and lost each other, only to find each other again. Now, as time passed, they both carried a quiet hope within them that someday, just as they had lost and found each other once, they would lose each other again and find their way back. It was a belief that, no matter the distance or time apart, fate would somehow bring them together once more".

www.ingramcontent.com/pod-product-compliance
Lightning Source LLC
Chambersburg PA
CBHW020623160726
47991CB00002BA/907